This book
belongs to:

MIGUEL
XXXANDXXX
SOCORRO

Disney · PIXAR

COCO

I Love My Family!

A Book of Memories

By

Miguel Rivera

For my little sister

Random House 🏠 New York

Dear Socorro,

I'm so happy you're finally here! This is my first time being a  big brother. To be honest, I'm a little nervous. Papá and Mamá said that I should set a good example for you because you'll be looking up to me. I'll do my best to be a good brother! There's a lot that I can tell you, but there's one thing I know best: our family.

I have so many stories to share with you! Some are happy, or funny, or sad—and some are magical! But they will all show you what makes our family

special. So here it is, our family album. I've made it for you so you will always remember who you are and where you come from.

Love,
Miguel

This is me!

Miguel Rivera

How to be a great musician:

- Practice, practice, practice!
- Listen to music that inspires you. Listen to it over and over again until you know it by heart!
- Find a great teacher who can help and encourage you.
- Never give up—even when things seem impossible.
- Did I mention you have to practice?

I have one big passion in life, but our family didn't always approve. I had to keep it a secret. Our family used to say I should stop daydreaming and keep my mind on shoemaking (our family business). That's fine for some people, but I want to be a musician more than anything! You're probably wondering why our relatives didn't like music. You'll have to wait. It's a great story!

I want to teach you to play the guitar one day!
These are all the important parts to know:

body

bridge

tuning pegs

frets

strings

sound
hole

One day I'll
write a song
for you!

I made this guitar
all by myself! I don't
have it anymore,
though. I'll tell you
about that later. . . .

Now that I think of it, my love of music wasn't a complete secret. I did tell someone. Does a dog count as a someone? This is my best friend, Dante. For a long time, Dante was my only audience. Sometimes he was also my backup singer! But Dante was a secret, too. Since he's a street dog, our family didn't want him around. I know what you're thinking—our family didn't seem to enjoy anything. Sometimes I thought they were shoemaking robots!

SHOES

Don't worry. A lot has changed since you came along.

Dante

But I have a lot more to tell you before we get to that story!

This is our home and business, Rivera Family Shoemakers. It may not look like much, but our family has been living and working here for generations.

huarache

wingtip

RIVERA
FAMILY
SHOEMAKERS
EST. 1921

boot →

Shoemaking has become the family tradition. Our parents make shoes, their parents made shoes, and their parents—you guessed it—made shoes. We make wingtips, boots, huaraches—any type of shoe you can think of. Well, as long as they aren't related to music in any way.

Papá says that shoemaking is in our blood. He's probably right, but I know that music is in _my_ blood. To practice my music, I used to go to my top-secret hideout in the attic. It was the place where I could be myself.

ofrenda room

Dante always sneaks into my hideout!

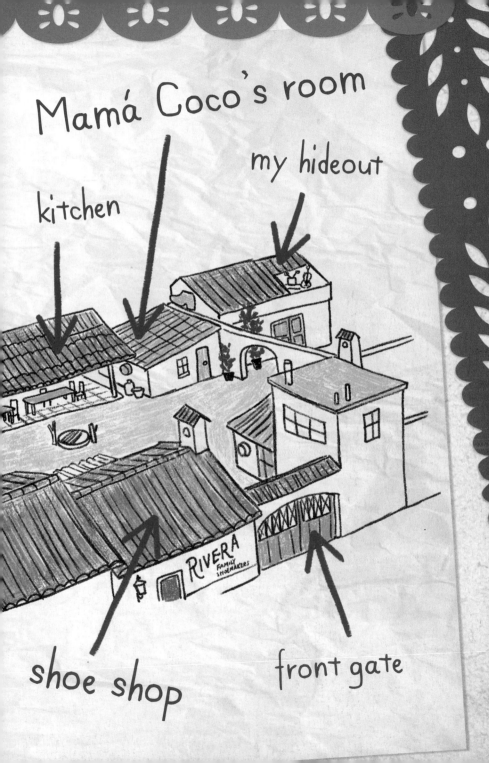

Santa Cecilia

This is Santa Cecilia, Mexico! Our town is little, but it's the <u>best</u> place to live. It has a plaza at the center, an old church with a bell tower that has a beautiful view, and great food on every corner. There are shops that sell everything from flowers and costumes to ice cream and cookies! My favorite place is Mariachi Plaza. No surprise there, right? It's where I would go to shine shoes and hear the best músicos in town. I hoped that one day I would perform in the plaza.

This is Mariachi Plaza.

The

These are some of the things
I love to do with my family.

Riveras

We're all different in many ways,
but we love each other so much.

What are some of your favorite family activities?

Abuelita

Our grandmother, Elena, is the head of the family. I just call her Abuelita. She is kind, hardworking, and tough as nails. We all do as she says because she has a good throwing arm and lots of shoes—and she is not afraid to use them! One time, Abuelita stormed down to Mariachi Plaza to chase away a musician who was talking to me. He didn't know what hit him! Abuelita and I don't always understand each other, but I know she only wants to protect me and our family.

shoe →

NO MUSIC!

← muscles

Papá Franco

Abuelita's husband
and our grandfather

There's no one calmer than Papá Franco.
He says that he and Abuelita are a perfect
balance: he is calm and easygoing, while Abuelita
is energetic and outspoken. Whenever I need some
peace and quiet, I go to Papá Franco.

Papá

This is Papá! He was so excited when he told me I would start making shoes with the family. He'll probably be just as excited for you to learn! Tip: He is the one to go to when Mamá doesn't want to take us out for ice cream (but don't tell Mamá!).

Mamá

Mamá is the best mom in the world (but you knew that already). She is really nice and patient, unless you haven't cleaned your room in two weeks. She tells great bedtime stories. She never gets tired of reading to all the kids in our family—even when we ask for the same stories over and over again!

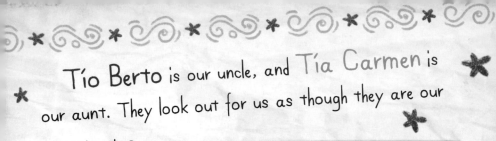

Tío Berto is our uncle, and Tía Carmen is our aunt. They look out for us as though they are our parents, too.

Tía Gloria is Papá's younger sister. She's lots of fun and loves to laugh. But she spends way too much time getting ready and hogs the bathroom.

Abel, Rosa, Manny, and Benny

These are our cousins: Abel, Rosa, Benny, and Manny. Their parents are Tío Berto and Tía Carmen. Abel is the oldest, and he loves playing fútbol. He is really goofy and likes to joke around. Rosa is next. She's only a couple years older than me, but she thinks she's the boss. She was super excited when you were born because there was finally another girl in the house. She's fun and adventurous. Benny and Manny are twins. They were the babies of the family until you came along. They may be cute, but they're troublemakers. Our house is busy with all our cousins around, but at least we always have someone to hang out with!

Mamá Coco was Abuelita's mother and our great-grandmother. She's no longer here, but her memory is still with us. We loved Mamá Coco so much that we named you after her! (Coco was her nickname—her real name was Socorro.) She didn't speak a lot as she got older, but we had fun together.

Mamá Coco

I told her everything and we played games all the time. I wish you could have met her, but I'll be sure to tell you lots of stories about her.

Who do you look forward to seeing at family gatherings?

This is all the family you've met so far. There are lots of others—you'll meet them later!

Mamá Coco

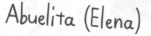

Abuelita (Elena)

Papá Franco

Tía Gloria

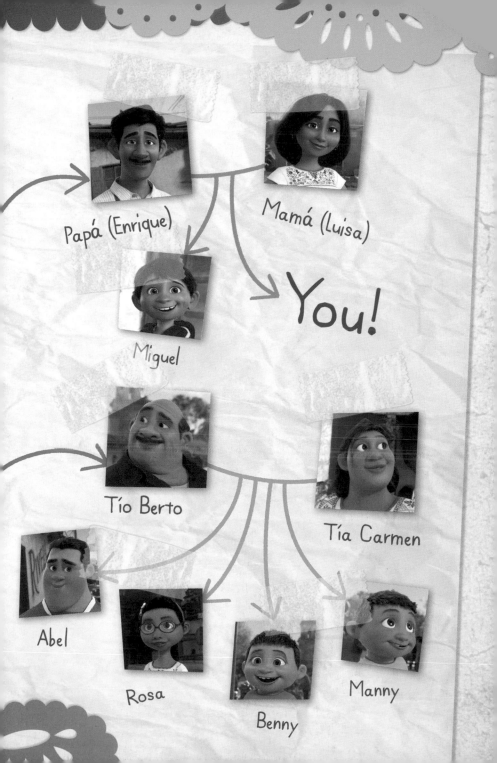

Papá (Enrique)

Mamá (Luisa)

You!

Miguel

Tío Berto

Tía Carmen

Abel

Rosa

Benny

Manny

The family legacy

Okay, I'm finally ready to tell our family story. I promise I'm not joking this time! It started a long time ago, back when Mamá Coco was a baby. The story is crazier than the telenovelas Mamá watches! Ready?

Once there was a family who lived in Santa Cecilia. The husband was a musician who decided to play music for the world. He left his wife and baby behind. That wife was Mamá Imelda, our great-great-grandmother, and the baby was Mamá Coco. After Mamá Imelda's husband left, she had to support her daughter on her own. So she started making shoes and built the family business.

For a long time, no one talked about Mamá Imelda's husband. All I knew was that he chose music over his family. That's where it started. After that, music was banned from our home.

Our relatives believed that if music destroyed our family once, it could happen again. Now you can see what I was up against. I could never be a musician because of something that had happened before I was born. It was so unfair! But then everything changed one day, on Día de los Muertos. . . .

Who is this guy?

Día de los Muertos

Every year on November 1st and 2nd, we celebrate Día de los Muertos, or Day of the Dead. We remember our ancestors who have died. Abuelita is always in charge of setting up the ofrenda. That's an altar full of photographs where we leave offerings of food, flowers, and all the stuff our relatives loved when they were alive. It looks amazing!

Next, we set up a path of marigolds to lead our ancestors' spirits from the cemetery to the ofrenda. Without the marigolds, they wouldn't know where to go!

The whole town is decorated for the celebration. There's papel picado everywhere! Papel picado decorations have beautiful designs cut into them. They are so colorful and bright! I like to walk around town to look at them.

Later, we go to the cemetery to set up candles and food for our loved ones. Some people may feel sad when they go to a cemetery, but on Día de los Muertos, everyone is full of happiness. The cemetery comes alive with the decorations, lights, and families gathered together to celebrate. We take turns telling stories and remembering our ancestors.

We prepare all this stuff for the dead, but there's lots for the living, too! My favorite thing is the pan de muerto. When Abuelita bakes this sweet bread, you can smell it from a mile away! It means "bread of the dead," but I still eat it! We also drink hot chocolate and atole, which tastes like vanilla and cinnamon.

atole

pan de muerto

¡Qué bueno!

I didn't know how important Día de los Muertos was until this absolutely crazy thing happened to me. You're about to hear a story so out of this world, even I wouldn't believe it if it hadn't happened to me. You have to promise not to tell anyone. Promise? Okay, here we go. . . .

On Día de los Muertos, I discovered that a folded photograph of Mamá Imelda showed a guitar. And it wasn't just any guitar . . . it was the guitar of **Ernesto de la Cruz!** Back then, he was the most famous musician in Mexico. I wanted to be just like him. I knew every song, every movie, everything he had ever created. He was <u>the guy</u>, you know?

So when I saw this guitar in the photo, I knew: Ernesto de la Cruz was my great-great-grandfather! But when I told our family, they freaked out! Abuelita found my secret hideout and smashed my guitar. I was hoping to perform in a special talent show that night, but without a guitar, it would be impossible. I was so mad at my family that I ran off to find another one. Ernesto de la Cruz said that you should seize your moment—and I knew this was mine.

I decided to borrow Ernesto de la Cruz's guitar from his tomb at the cemetery. I know I shouldn't have taken something from a grave. But I wouldn't have done it if it hadn't been an emergency!

He was my great-great-grandfather, so I thought he would've wanted me to have it. When I played the guitar, a bunch of marigold petals flew up and floated all around me. And when I went outside, there were skeletons everywhere! Maybe taking the guitar wasn't a good idea. . . .

BIENVENIDOS

I know it sounds impossible, but I promise I'm not lying: I went to the Land of the Dead! It was connected to the land of the living by a beautiful bridge made of marigolds. The spirits could cross the bridge to visit their families only on Día de los Muertos. There were hundreds of skeletons crossing the bridge and bringing back all the food and drinks their living relatives had left for them.

I couldn't believe the Land of the Dead was a huge and busy city! The buildings went high into the sky, and trains and trolleys traveled up, down, and across the city.

In the center was Plaza de la Cruz, named in honor of—you guessed it—Ernesto de la Cruz. He also had the coolest mansion! Everyone hoped they would get invited to his parties.

Even though it was called the Land of the Dead, the city was full of color and life. But there was a place that was not so bright. This was where the almost-forgotten spirits hung out. They didn't have a photo on any ofrenda in the Land of the Living, so they couldn't cross the Marigold Bridge. It was sad to see these people without their families on Día de los Muertos, but they seemed to have fun together.

Some of the most incredible things I saw were the spirit creatures. They looked like the alebrije art I'd seen in shops in Santa Cecilia. In the Land of the Dead, the spirit creatures guided souls on their journeys. They were made of different colors and animals. Some had claws, horns, beaks, and even wings.

wings

horns

tail

claws

I made this drawing of Pepita for school. My classmates have no idea that she's real!

Pepita by Miguel

What would your spirit guide look like?

During my adventure, I met Pepita. She seemed big and scary at first, but we became friends.

The biggest surprise was that Dante became my spirit guide after he helped me on my journey. He seemed so happy to fly around with Pepita.

He's a good boy!

Dante!

While I was in the Land of the Dead, I met our ancestors! I had only thought of them as photos on the ofrenda, but when I got to meet them, I realized how unique each of them was.

Tío Felipe and Tío Óscar

Tío Felipe and Tío Óscar are Mamá Imelda's younger brothers. As you can see, they are identical twins. They know each other so well that they finish each other's sentences. They are much taller than I thought they'd be.

Papá Julio

This is Papá Julio, Mamá Coco's husband. He panics easily, but he's kind and caring. He always thinks of the family's best interests.

Tía Rosita

Tía Rosita is Papá Julio's sister. She was the first family member I met after I took Ernesto de la Cruz's guitar. She gave me the biggest hug. She's friendly and smiles a lot.

Tía Victoria

Tía Victoria is Papá Julio and Mamá Coco's daughter. She is **super smart** and says what's on her mind. She wasn't very happy when she found out I took Ernesto's guitar from his grave, but she still wanted to help me and our family.

Mamá Imelda

And last but not least, there's Mamá Imelda. She is Mamá Coco's mother and my great-great-grandmother. She's pretty cool—she started the family shoemaking business all by herself! By passing down a skill, she made sure no one in our family would struggle like she once did. We owe her a lot. But it was hard that her ban on music affected the whole family—for generations! She didn't understand when she found out that I love music. In order to return home, I needed a **blessing** from someone in my family. Mamá Imelda would only give her blessing if I promised never to play music again. That didn't seem fair to me, so I decided to take matters into my own hands. . . .

This is what Mamá Imelda looks like in the Land of the Dead.

Is there an amazing woman in your life who you admire?

In the Land of the Dead, I also met Hector. Hector was slowly being forgotten. If no one remembered him in the Land of the Living, he would fade away from the Land of the Dead. I wanted to help Hector, but I had to find Ernesto de la Cruz first. I needed his blessing in order to return home and finally become a musician! So Hector and I made a deal: he would help me get to Ernesto, and I would put Hector's photo on the ofrenda when I went back home.

It turned out that Hector was a musician, too. To get to Ernesto, we had to win a talent show so we could perform at his mansion. I was so nervous that I almost chickened out, but Hector taught me how to do a loud shout called a grito. It grabbed the audience's attention, and we had fun singing and dancing together. But before we found out who won the talent show, we had an argument, so I had to find Ernesto de la Cruz all by myself.

When I finally got to the mansion, the thing I had never thought possible actually happened. I **sang for Ernesto de la Cruz!** I was confident and smooth, just like he was . . . until I fell into the pool. At least I made a **splash!**

Ernesto was shocked when he found out he had a great-great-grandson. But once I told him, he showed me around his mansion and introduced me to his friends. He seemed like the coolest guy. He was about to give me his blessing, but suddenly, Hector burst into the room.

You should sit down for this, because here is when things got CRAZY. I found out that when they were alive, Ernesto de la Cruz and Hector were best friends. Hector wrote songs and Ernesto performed them. They were the perfect team. Until one day, Hector decided to quit and return to his family. Ernesto got so angry that he poisoned Hector! With Hector gone, Ernesto could steal his music and take all the glory for himself. Ernesto de la Cruz was not the hero everyone thought he was.

Did you see that coming? I didn't!

Now, you might be worried that we're related to a very evil man. But I found out that there was only one person Hector wanted to see in the whole world: his daughter, Coco. Yep, that's right. He was talking about our great-grandmother, Mamá Coco. Hector is our great-great-grandfather!

Ernesto de la Cruz's biggest hit, "Remember Me," was actually written by Hector for Mamá Coco. When Coco was a little girl, they would sing it together. He wanted her to know how much he loved her.

Remember
Me

When Mamá Imelda found out that Hector had tried to return to her and Coco, she forgave him. She also gave me her blessing to go back home—with no conditions. But I needed to get to Mamá Coco fast. She was forgetting Hector, so he was starting to disappear!

At first, Mamá Coco didn't seem to understand anything I was saying. But then I sang "Remember Me" to her. The song started to bring back memories of her papá, and she sang with me! Then she told us a bunch of stories about her papá. Hector was saved!

Now there's a spot in our home where we celebrate Hector's music. Lots of people come to visit! We also have a photo of Papá Hector on our ofrenda so he can visit us every Día de los Muertos. And best of all, we have music to bring us together.

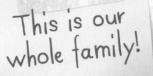

This is our whole family!

I had to ask Mamá and Papá for help with this. We have a big family!

Papá Hector

Mamá Imelda

Tío Óscar

Tío Felipe

Mamá Coco

Papá Julio

Tía Rosita

Tía Victoria

Abuelita (Elena)

Papá Franco

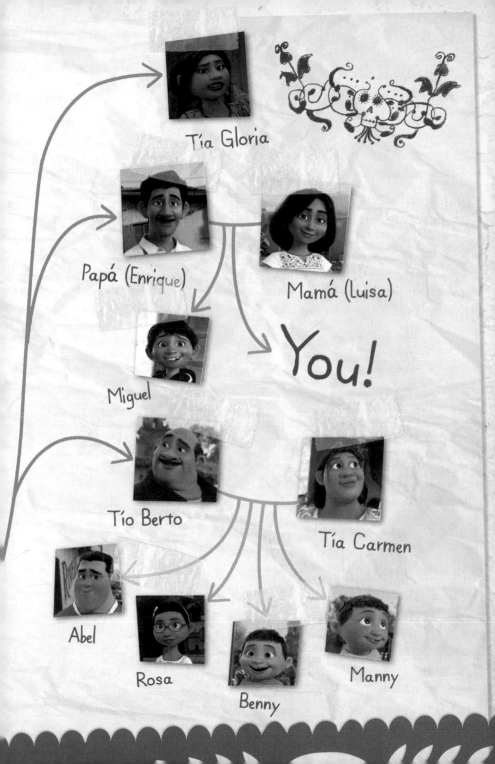

Tía Gloria

Papá (Enrique)

Mamá (Luisa)

You!

Miguel

Tío Berto

Tía Carmen

Abel

Rosa

Benny

Manny

I learned a lot about our family and about myself during my adventure. I used to feel like an outsider in my own family because of my love of music. But now I see that music is what brought us together in the first place—and it's the thing that connects us even now. I hope you find your passion one day, too! It might be shoes, music, or something completely different.

Maybe you'll be a writer!

The BEST Book EVER! by Socorro R.

Or a famous fútbol player!

RIVERA

Or an astronaut!

I know I still have a lot to learn (I'm only thirteen, after all!), but I have some advice:

- Never underestimate the love your family has for you.

- Respect your elders (especially your big brother). Their experiences may save you in more ways than one!

- Don't give up on your dreams. If you work hard and believe in yourself, maybe they'll come true!

- Be nice to stray dogs. They might just be magical creatures!

- Show your love for those around you every day. They won't be here forever.

- Share stories about the people you love the most.

What advice would you give to a younger person? What stories would you share?

By
Edlin Ortiz

Illustrated by
the Disney Storybook Art Team

A special thanks to Adrian Molina, Melissa Bernabei,
Marcela Davison Aviles, and the Coco Art Department

Designed by Tony Fejeran

Visit us on the Web!
randomhousekids.com

Educators and librarians, for a variety of teaching tools, visit us at
RHTeachersLibrarians.com

ISBN 978-0-7364-3847-6
Printed in the United States of America
10 9 8 7 6 5 4 3 2